Undercover
published in 2008 by
Hardie Grant Egmont
85 High Street
Prahran, Victoria 3181, Australia
www.hardiegrantegmont.com.au

A CiP record for this title is available from the National Library of Australia

Text copyright © 2008 H.I. Larry
Illustration and design copyright © 2008 Hardie Grant Egmont

Cover and illustrations by Andy Hook
Based on original illustration and design by Ash Oswald
Typeset by Pauline Haas

Printed in Australia by McPherson's Printing Group

1 3 5 7 9 10 8 6 4 2

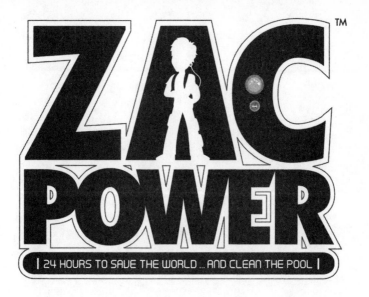

ZAC POWER™

| 24 HOURS TO SAVE THE WORLD ... AND CLEAN THE POOL |

UNDERCOVER
BY **H. I. LARRY**

ILLUSTRATIONS BY ANDY HOOK

CHAPTER... ...ONE

Zac Power watched as the volleyball flew over the net towards him. It was a perfect set-up, but Zac knew he should miss the shot on purpose.

He sighed as the volleyball flew past.

'Zac,' called Mr Kane, his PE teacher, 'don't be afraid of the ball!'

Zac went red. He hated this part of his life. He hated having to pretend that he was terrible in PE, even though really he was brilliant at sports.

Nobody was allowed to know that Zac Power was actually a spy for the Government Investigation Bureau, or GIB for short. Nobody was allowed to know that he could pilot the latest jet fighters. Or that he had set a new record for deep-sea exploration in a mini-sub. Or that he had taken a top-secret shuttle into space.

'Sorry, Mr Kane,' Zac muttered.

'Nobody can be good at everything, right?' said Mr Kane, shaking his head.

Zac turned away so that Mr Kane wouldn't see him rolling his eyes. *If only he knew what I could really do!*

But just then something caught his attention. He was sure he could hear the faint sound of an engine – coming from just outside the gym, in the change room. Zac's spy senses tingled.

He started jogging towards the change room, calling over his shoulder, 'Mr Kane, I'm just going to the toilet!'

Before Mr Kane could reply, Zac had charged into the change room and shut the door behind him.

'Hey,' said his brother Leon. 'That was quick! I only just got here.'

Zac raised his eyebrows and grinned. Leon was sitting inside a strange-looking vehicle with three wheels.

The curved glass roof was open and pointing upwards.

'You better get in,' said Leon, revving the engine. 'I'm supposed to take you there straight away.'

Leon was also a spy for GIB, but instead of being a field agent like Zac, he was in charge of technology back at the office.

'Take me where?' asked Zac. He yanked his backpack off its peg and slid into the passenger's seat. 'And what *is* this thing?'

'This *thing*,' said Leon proudly, 'is my latest invention, the Triox. It runs entirely on household rubbish!'

'You mean it's like a recycling machine?' said Zac, impressed.

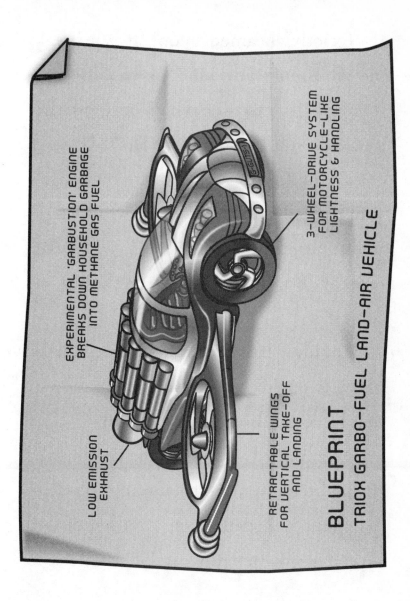

BLUEPRINT
TRIOX GARBO-FUEL LAND-AIR VEHICLE

EXPERIMENTAL 'GARBUSTION' ENGINE
BREAKS DOWN HOUSEHOLD GARBAGE
INTO METHANE GAS FUEL

3-WHEEL-DRIVE SYSTEM
FOR MOTORCYCLE-LIKE
LIGHTNESS & HANDLING

LOW EMISSION
EXHAUST

RETRACTABLE WINGS
FOR VERTICAL TAKE-OFF
AND LANDING

Exactly,' beamed Leon. 'It can break down almost any kind of rubbish and convert it into gas which powers the vehicle. Now, give me your SpyPad.'

Zac pulled his SpyPad out of his pocket and handed it to Leon. The SpyPad was a multi-purpose communication gadget that every GIB agent had to keep on them at all times.

Zac loved his SpyPad. Not only could he use it to download his favourite TV shows, but he could also play games on it.

Leon pulled a lever on the dashboard. Behind them, on the back of the Triox, a hatch flipped open. Leon leant out of the driver's side window and tossed Zac's

SpyPad over his shoulder into the recycling unit. The unit spun madly, crunching the gadget up into tiny pieces.

'What are you doing, Leon?' Zac said. 'That's GIB-issued. I need that for my missions!'

'I'll explain it all on the way,' said Leon. He pointed to a safety harness. 'Strap yourself in!'

CHAPTER... ...TWO

Leon reversed the Triox and zoomed out the back door of the gym building, outside onto the oval. Zac had just finished strapping on his harness when he realised that Leon was heading straight towards the solid brick wall of the girls' toilets.

Zac flattened himself against the seat and braced himself for impact...but then the Triox lifted into the air!

Zac looked out his window and saw two wide, flat panels swinging out from under the Triox. The wings locked into place as the vehicle soared through the air.

Zac glanced over at the altitude indicator. In four seconds, they had risen over 500 metres. *Not bad,* he thought.

'OK,' said Zac, leaning back in his seat. 'What's with scrapping my SpyPad?'

'Right, sorry,' said Leon. He pulled a gleaming red gadget from his pocket and tossed it at Zac.

'That's the new Pulsetronic V-66, the very latest SpyPad model. We've boosted the ultra-violet scanner, and tweaked the microscope and nightscope.'

'Cool,' said Zac, turning the shiny new SpyPad over in his hands.

'We had to destroy the old Turbo 3000 range because they were infected by a scrambling virus,' said Leon. 'Unfortunately, the virus was sent this morning, so you never received your mission.'

'Hang on – I'm supposed to be on a mission right now?'

Leon nodded. 'You were supposed to have started hours ago. Headquarters had to send me to collect you in person.'

'What's going on?' said Zac, surprised. He'd never been to HQ before.

'Read the message on your new Pulsetronic V-66,' said Leon grimly.

CLASSIFIED

MESSAGE INITIATED 12:00PM
CURRENT TIME 4:00PM

Welcome to your new
Pulsetronic V-66 SpyPad.

GIB has reason to believe that
there is a double agent working
inside the Headquarters of GIB.

This is extremely dangerous
because at noon tomorrow, the
yearly global back-up of all GIB
computers will take place.

This process cannot be stopped!
All top-secret files will be vulnerable
to download by the intruder for a
period of five minutes. Your mission is
to track down the unidentified spy and
arrest him.

MISSION TIME REMAINING: 20 HOURS

END

'If the mole hacks into the system during the back-up, GIB could be destroyed!' exclaimed Zac.

'Exactly,' said Leon. 'Here, you'd better take over the Triox while I fill you in.'

The dashboard slid open on Zac's side of the Triox, revealing a second set of controls. Zac gripped the controls and pulled them towards him.

'How do I get to HQ?' said Zac.

'You don't need to know,' said Leon. 'The secret location coordinates have already been entered into the GPS system. You just need to steer the controls.'

Leon pushed his glasses up his nose and cleared his throat loudly.

Zac rolled his eyes. He knew how much his brother loved a mission briefing.

'Now, we're not sure yet whether this mole is one of our own spies turned bad,' began Leon, 'or a BIG spy that's managed to get into HQ.'

BIG were GIB's sworn enemies. They were an evil spy organisation that had tried every scheme in the book to cause global disasters, steal millions and destroy GIB.

'Not knowing who the mole is at GIB makes this mission even more dangerous,' Leon continued. 'Which is why Agent Big Boss, the head of GIB, requested you for this job. He's been very impressed with your missions so far.'

'Oh, I see,' said Zac, trying not to look too pleased.

'Speaking of special requests,' added Leon with a smile, 'mum says it's your turn to clean the pool when you get back.'

'Great,' groaned Zac. He hated cleaning the grubby pool filter, but he pushed the thought from his mind. 'By the way, how do we know there's a mole at GIB? No-one has ever cracked HQ security.'

'Someone's cracked it now,' said Leon. 'This morning we tracked a number of strange, coded messages from HQ to BIG. We cracked the code and discovered that the virus that scrambled all the SpyPads was sent from inside GIB.'

'No GIB agent would do that,' said Zac. He forced the controls towards the dashboard, and the Triox picked up speed.

'I know,' said Leon. 'To make matters worse, all this brand new equipment has been stolen from our Advanced Research Lab. Hey, we're almost at HQ!'

Zac felt the controls pull away as the Triox moved into auto-pilot. The vehicle suddenly swooped towards the ground, flying in the direction of an almost-empty car park.

Zac craned his neck to look for the GIB HQ among the buildings in the city streets, but he couldn't see it anywhere.

They wouldn't make their HQ in a car park, would they? he wondered.

But the Triox continued down towards the car park. It was heading straight for a rusty-looking caravan.

A caravan? thought Zac, confused.

'We're here,' said Leon. 'Welcome to HQ!'

CHAPTER... ...THREE

The Triox dropped and hovered in the air, just above the old wreck.

Zac looked doubtfully at Leon.

Leon pressed a small button on the dashboard. 'Look down again, Zac.'

Zac glanced down. To his surprise, the caravan had vanished. *That's so clever,* thought Zac. *A decoy hologram protects the entrance to HQ.*

Underneath where the hologram had been just moments before, heavy steel trap doors were parting slowly. Zac could see bright lights shining from underground.

The Triox then lowered into the ground, and the metal doors clanked shut above them.

Zac pulled off his safety harness and opened the glass roof of the Triox. The vehicle hummed to a stop and the wings folded away underneath the vehicle.

Zac gazed around HQ Level 1. It was massive, the size of an aircraft hangar. There were hi-tech choppers, cars, jets, boats and motorbikes lined up as far as the eye could see.

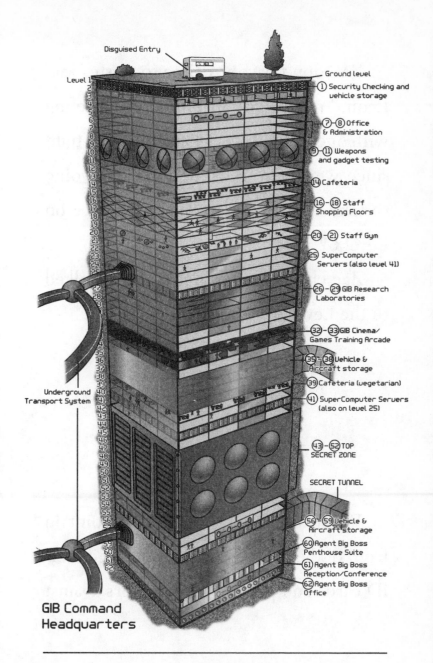

Disguised Entry

Ground level

Level 1

① Security Checking and vehicle storage

⑦–⑧ Office & Administration

⑨–⑪ Weapons and gadget testing

⑭ Cafeteria

⑯–⑱ Staff Shopping Floors

⑳–㉑ Staff Gym

㉕ SuperComputer Servers (also level 41)

㉖–㉙ GIB Research Laboratories

㉜–㉝ GIB Cinema/ Games Training Arcade

㉟–㊳ Vehicle & Aircraft storage

㊴ Cafeteria (vegetarian)

㊶ SuperComputer Servers (also on level 25)

㊸–㊼ TOP SECRET ZONE

SECRET TUNNEL

㊻–㊾ Vehicle & Aircraft storage

㊿ Agent Big Boss Penthouse Suite

㊱ Agent Big Boss Reception/Conference

㊲ Agent Big Boss Office

Underground Transport System

GIB Command Headquarters

·•| 19 |•·

'We don't have any time to waste,' said Leon. 'You've got an important briefing with Agent Big Boss. Security is extra tight since we discovered the mole. It's going to take ages to get down to his office on Level 62.'

Zac checked his watch as they walked to the Level 1 checkpoint.

When they got to the checkpoint in front of the lift, Leon and Zac swiped their ID cards and pressed their fingers against the security check-pad. Then they spoke their names into the database microphone, and had their faces scanned.

'We'll have to do that every time we enter or leave a floor,' groaned Leon as the lift doors hissed shut. 'And it'll only get worse when we get to Agent Big Boss' floor!'

At Level 62, the lift doors opened to a swarm of GIB guards.

Zac and Leon presented their ID cards for scanning. They had to pass through an X-ray machine and a metal detector. Then they were both patted down for weapons.

Zac and Leon were then marched down a short hallway by four armed guards. They stopped outside a reinforced steel door, and one of the guards pressed the buzzer.

After a moment, the steel door slid open.

'Hello, agents,' said a short, dark man. 'I'm Agent Big Boss.'

'I'm Agent Rock Star, sir,' said Zac.

'Good to meet you, Rock Star,' rumbled Agent Big Boss in a deep voice. 'And nice to see you again, Agent Tech Head.'

'Hi,' said Leon nervously.

Agent Big Boss gestured for the boys to sit down as the guards headed back into the hallway. Behind them, the heavy steel door slid shut.

'I really appreciate your working on this mission, Rock Star,' said Agent Big Boss. 'It would be disastrous for GIB if this mole succeeds in hacking into the system.'

Zac nodded. He looked around the office at some of the most advanced technological protection in the world. There were plasma screens showing security vision from every level of HQ. Super-strength titanium shielding on the walls curved into the ceiling.

Then Zac noticed something odd. The panel that covered the air-conditioning vent was missing two screws. Suddenly Zac had the peculiar, uncomfortable feeling that he was being watched.

Probably just the security cameras, he thought, pushing the feeling to one side.

'You can run this investigation any way you want,' Agent Big Boss said. 'But you'll have to keep it *completely* secret. How are you planning to start?'

'First I'll have to narrow down our suspects,' said Zac, thinking fast. 'And then

I'll need to find a way to question them without letting on that they are a suspect, to protect the secrecy of the mission.'

Leon spoke up. 'I have a gadget that might be useful for you, then.'

Zac and Agent Big Boss turned to Leon.

'It's called the FF-Matrix, short for Face & Form Matrix Appearance Altering Apparatus,' explained Leon. 'It's a micro-chip that you attach to your clothing. It uses your body heat to send out holographic micro-pulses. It's not quite ready for use yet, but –'

'Sounds good,' interrupted Zac. 'But what does it actually do?'

'Well,' said Leon, 'it disguises you with

a mobile hologram. You can change your appearance by adjusting the FF-Matrix settings on your new SpyPad.'

'Perfect,' said Zac, standing up. 'We'd better get a move on.'

'Good luck, agents,' said Agent Big Boss in his deep voice. He pressed a big red button on his desk and the steel door behind them slid open. 'GIB is counting on you.'

CHAPTER... ...FOUR

The lift doors opened at Level 27, where Leon's office in the Advanced Research Lab was located. Leon and Zac had to swipe their ID cards and submit to security checks before they could even leave the lift.

'Leon, as soon as we get to your office, I'll need access to the GIB Agent Database,' said Zac as he held his head in front of the security scanner.

A red laser flashed over his face, and then a green light blinked. 'I want to run background checks on any GIB agents that have been acting weirdly lately.'

'That sounds good,' said Leon, 'because I'd like to run some tests on the FF-Matrix.'

Zac followed Leon into his lab, and sat down at Leon's work station. As Leon worked on a tangle of wires and tiny electronic parts, Zac logged on to the Agent Database.

If I were a mole, thought Zac, *where would I hide at GIB?*

He printed out a list of the items stolen from the Advanced Research Lab, and began running searches through the database.

Next, Zac clicked through the files of hundreds of GIB agents. He cross-checked security reports, looking for clues, and gradually built up a short list of suspects to investigate.

Finally! thought Zac. *It's time to go mole hunting.* He checked his watch.

'Hey, Leon,' Zac called across the lab. 'I'm ready to start moving.'

Leon looked up from his work. 'Just give me a couple more minutes. I couldn't find my final version of the FF-Matrix, so I had to rig another one up from scratch.' Leon came over to where Zac was working. 'What have you found out?' he whispered.

'Well, I have two prime suspects,' said Zac in a low voice, checking over his shoulder that no-one was listening. 'The first is a guy called Agent Checkmate. Apparently, GIB have been tailing him for two months because he was spotted secretly meeting with BIG's knife-fighting expert, Switchblade. It's possible Switchblade bribed Checkmate to become a double agent.'

'And suspect number two?' asked Leon, carefully snipping some wires.

'A guy called Agent Test Tube,' said Zac. 'He works here in the Advanced Research Lab. Could have stolen the equipment.'

'Interesting,' said Leon thoughtfully. 'I really like Test Tube, but he does get teased for being a crazy scientist.'

'Exactly,' said Zac. 'Maybe he's fed up with it. The teasing has gotten worse lately because he's been working on a gadget called the Intelligent Jelly Corrosive Acid Bomb.'

Zac leant on the lab bench, thinking hard. 'Speaking of crazy gadgets,' he said, 'what are the ScavMod and the TeraStick? They're on the list of stolen inventions, but I've never heard of them.'

'That's because they're brand new,' said Leon. 'The mole stole our prototypes. The ScavMod is a micro-computer designed to crack passwords. It can hack into a network and transmit files for storage to the TeraStick, which is the most powerful memory stick ever created. The two gadgets can be disguised together as any small, everyday item – like a piece of fruit, or an asthma pump.'

For the first time that day, Zac suddenly felt nervous. *That means the mole has everything he needs to steal all of GIB's most valuable secrets during the global back-up*, he realised. *And the identity of every GIB spy could be made public!*

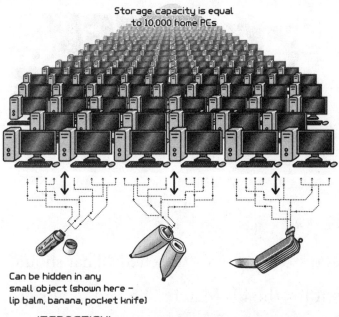

Storage capacity is equal
to 10,000 home PCs

Can be hidden in any
small object (shown here –
lip balm, banana, pocket knife)

'TERASTICK' – holds 1000 TERABYTES of memory in stick

As if he could read Zac's thoughts, Leon nodded and said, 'That mole has everything he needs to destroy GIB.'

CHAPTER... ...FIVE

Leon stood up and stretched. 'That should do it for the FF-Matrix,' he said. 'Let's get you rigged up!'

Zac stood still as Leon carefully stuck a tiny chip underneath his shirt.

'Thanks, Leon,' he said. 'I'm going to check on Agent Checkmate first. Database security tracking says that he's down in the Weapons Testing and Combat Training

Zone on Level 10. I'll try and get him talking while we practise, and see if he lets anything slip.'

'Be careful, Zac,' said Leon. 'The hologram will look solid, but if you come into contact with anything, it'll distort. Checkmate will know at once that you're in disguise.'

Not if I can help it, thought Zac.

He and Leon headed out of the lab to the lift. Once they got there, they had to go through all the security checks again.

I know GIB can't take any chances with security if there's a mole on the loose, thought Zac, *but this is becoming a major hassle.* He checked his watch, feeling impatient.

Eventually the lights flashed green, and the lift doors opened. Leon and Zac ducked into the Level 10 toilets.

'You should turn on the FF-Matrix now,' said Leon. 'You can control it with your SpyPad. I've loaded the identities of every GIB agent who matches your height. Who do you want to look like?'

Zac racked his brains. *I need to look like someone Checkmate has met before*, he thought, *but not someone he knows too well.*

'I know,' said Zac. 'Agent Lock Pick!'

'That guy who lives on junk food?' said Leon, raising an eyebrow.

'Yup,' said Zac. 'I had a pizza once with Lock Pick and Checkmate, just after we graduated from Spy Academy. Agent Lock Pick never stops talking, which is great because I'll need to ask Checkmate lots of questions.'

'Good thinking,' Leon said.

Zac grinned and punched in the selection into the appearance menu on his SpyPad. He then selected the tracksuit function.

As soon as he hit the enter key, he felt the hairs on the back of his neck stick straight up.

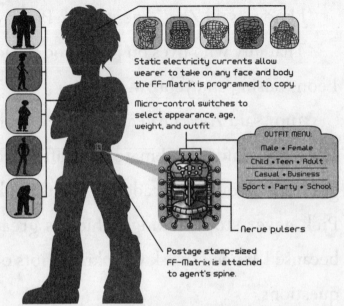

Static electricity currents allow wearer to take on any face and body the FF-Matrix is programmed to copy.

Micro-control switches to select appearance, age, weight, and outfit

OUTFIT MENU:
Male • Female
Child • Teen • Adult
Casual • Business
Sport • Party • School

Nerve pulsers

Postage stamp-sized FF-Matrix is attached to agent's spine.

FF-MATRIX (FACE AND FORM MATRIX APPEARANCE ALTERING APPARATUS)

Leon beamed. Zac looked at himself in the mirror and gasped.

Zac's face and body looked bigger, his hair was darker and longer, and now he was wearing a tracksuit. He looked exactly like Lock Pick!

Zac lifted his hand in amazement, and watched as the hologram of Lock Pick did the same in the mirror.

'It works by molding the hologram to your skin with static electricity,' Leon explained proudly. 'That's how it simulates natural movement.'

'Nice work, Leon,' Zac said, still staring at himself in the mirror.

'I don't know Lock Pick, so I'll wait for you back at the lab,' said Leon. 'Zac, be careful. If Checkmate is the mole and he realises that you're onto him, he might get desperate.'

'Don't worry,' said Zac, finally turning away from his reflection. 'I'm not taking any chances in the Weapons Testing and Combat Training Zone!'

Zac left the toilets and walked carefully down the hallway, trying to remember how Lock Pick moved. The FF-Matrix could only change his appearance so much. *I'll have to be careful about how I speak, too*, Zac realised. *The FF-Matrix can't change my voice.*

Zac stopped in front of the steel door of the training zone. He swiped his ID card and pushed it open.

The walls of the huge room were lined with complex equipment. There was a target range in one corner, and weapons lockers opposite. The floor was covered with mats for practising martial arts.

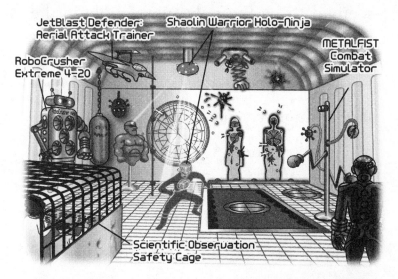

JetBlast Defender: Aerial Attack Trainer

Shaolin Warrior Holo-Ninja

METALFIST Combat Simulator

RoboCrusher Extreme 4-20

Scientific Observation Safety Cage

GIB HQ WEAPONS TESTING & COMBAT TRAINING ZONE

This has to be the coolest room at GIB HQ, Zac thought to himself. *I've got to come back here sometime!*

Zac caught sight of Agent Checkmate over at a MetalFist robotic boxing machine, and headed in his direction. Luckily, they seemed to be the only two people in the entire training zone.

'Hey, Checkmate,' called Zac, in a slightly higher voice.

'Hey,' replied Agent Checkmate. He stepped back from the MetalFist and wiped away some sweat. 'How are you, er –'

'Lock Pick,' Zac interrupted. 'We had pizza one night with Rock Star, remember?'

'Oh, right,' Checkmate said with a nod. 'Let me think…You were medium Hawaiian with triple pineapple, right? And Rock Star had spicy beef Mexicana with extra corn chips and sour cream.'

'Impressive!' said Zac.

'I'm not good with faces, but I never

forget a pizza!' Checkmate laughed, turning back to the boxing machine and raising his fists.

I've got to keep him talking! thought Zac quickly. *I need to turn the conversation to Switchblade...*

'So, Checkmate,' said Zac as he stretched his leg out on the mat. 'What do you do when you're not training? Hang out with friends?'

'Yeah, I guess,' puffed Checkmate, ducking a power punch from the MetalFist and hitting back. 'But I have a lot of homework, too.'

Zac nodded. 'I always find that only other spies can really understand how we're too busy for homework,' he said, trying to sound chatty. 'Are you friends with any other agents?'

Checkmate paused for a minute. There were beads of sweat running down his face. He turned to Zac, an eyebrow raised. 'Why do you want to know?'

Zac shrugged, trying to look bored. But before he could reply…

SPLAAAT!

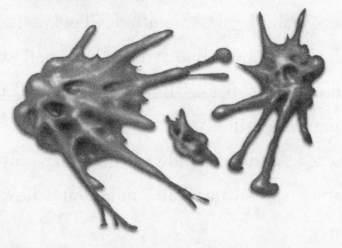

Huge globs of green goo were suddenly flying through the air. One of them had landed on Checkmate's face! The sticky slime started to harden as it oozed over the agent's mouth and nose.

'Checkmate!' Zac yelled, scrambling towards him.

But the agent's face was already turning blue. With his nose and mouth sealed shut, Checkmate couldn't breathe!

Zac watched in horror as Checkmate collapsed on the floor.

CHAPTER... ...SIX

Zac dropped to his knees and crawled over to Checkmate. He still didn't know where the green muck was coming from.

Before he could locate their attacker, there were more green blobs flying in his direction. Zac rolled onto the ground, but he wasn't fast enough. A huge glob of goo hit Zac square in the back, almost knocking the wind out of him.

He did a commando roll over to Checkmate. Staying low, Zac dragged the struggling agent over to the Scientific Observation Safety Cage, and slammed the hatch behind him.

'This is going to hurt,' Zac muttered, digging his fingers underneath the hard glob covering Checkmate's face.

Then Zac ripped the hard green blob off like an old bandaid.

'OUCH!' spluttered Checkmate, gasping for air and staring in shock at Zac. 'Agent Rock Star? Where did Lock Pick go? Is he…*dead?*'

'Um, I am Lock Pick,' Zac said, feeling around on his back for the FF-Matrix chip.

But his fingers only found sticky green goo. 'Right, sorry … I *was* Lock Pick, now I'm Rock Star.'

'*What* are you talking about?' said Checkmate, still breathing heavily.

'I'll explain later,' said Zac, trying to wipe the green goo off his fingers. It hardened and stuck fast to his jeans.

What's attacking us? he wondered, trying not to panic. *We're safe for now, but we can't stay in this cage forever…*

Then Zac realised that the weapons lockers were wide open. *When did that happen?* He scanned the room quickly.

There was group of robotic guns marching across the floor towards them!

Checkmate had dragged himself up next to Zac. 'Oh no!' he gasped. 'Those are SAG-11s!'

The robotic guns were firing as they moved. Fat globs of goo splattered against the outside of the cage.

'What are they?' Zac asked.

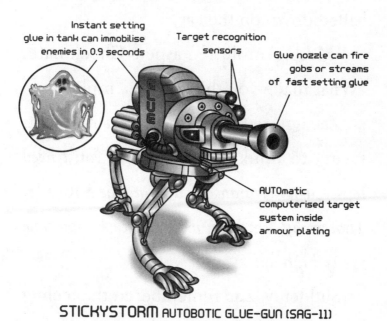

Instant setting glue in tank can immobilise enemies in 0.9 seconds

Target recognition sensors

Glue nozzle can fire gobs or streams of fast setting glue

AUTOmatic computerised target system inside armour plating

STICKYSTORM AUTOBOTIC GLUE-GUN (SAG-11)

'SAG-11s are StickyStorm Autobotic Glue-Guns!' said Checkmate wildly. 'They're operated by remote control and are programmed to suffocate their targets with sticky glue!'

'At least I know you're not the mole, now,' said Zac, ducking again as green goo hailed down on the cage.

'Me…a mole?!' gasped Checkmate. 'What made you think I was a mole?'

Zac ignored Checkmate for a moment, trying to think quickly. *Surely you'd need top-security clearance to activate the SAG-11s. That means that the mole has to be someone pretty high up!*

Suddenly, Zac remembered the feeling

of being watched in Agent Big Boss' office. *I should have listened to my instincts,* thought Zac. *I knew something wasn't right! Someone knows I'm in the building, and they're out to stop me.*

Then Zac had an idea. 'Checkmate,' he said quickly, 'how do you program the SAG-11s so they know who to hunt?'

'Um, lots of ways,' said Checkmate, leaning heavily against the cage wall. 'Sometimes they go by visual recognition, but that's not always reliable, so they search for ID chips –'

'Ah-ha!' yelled Zac, as more goo rained down on the cage. 'They're programmed to hunt my ID card! That's how they knew where I was, even though I was in disguise.'

Zac pulled Checkmate to his feet.

'When I say go,' said Zac firmly, 'you have to run to the exit.'

Checkmate went white. 'But –'

'One ...' Zac said, slowly pulling his ID card out of his pocket and pushing gently on the cage door. 'Two...*three!*'

Zac kicked open the cage door and flung his ID card into the far corner of the room. 'Run, Checkmate!'

The two agents bolted towards the exit as the SAG-11s swung towards the ID card and fired. A shower of green goo exploded in the corner of the training zone.

Zac sprinted out the door of the training zone, with Checkmate right behind him. He slammed the door shut and pulled out his SpyPad, dialing quickly.

'Leon!' Zac said, breathing heavily. 'You need to send a security and clean-up crew to the training zone right now.'

'What's wrong?' asked his brother. 'Did Checkmate do something?'

'Checkmate's not the mole!' Zac replied. 'We just got attacked by a group of SAG-11s.'

On the other end of the line, Leon made a choking noise. '*What?*'

After he'd hung up, Zac turned to Checkmate. 'You can head home if you want,' he said. 'I've got to wait here for the clean-up crew so I can get my ID back, and make sure the SAG-11s don't get loose.'

And complete my mission, he added silently, checking the time.

Agent Checkmate nodded. He was still white as a sheet. 'Thanks, Rock Star.'

Zac shrugged. 'Any time.' Then he remembered something. 'Hey, you're not a suspect anymore. But why have you been meeting up with Switchblade?'

Checkmate looked awkward for a moment. 'Er, Switchblade is my cousin,' he said. 'He works for BIG and I've been trying for years to get him to join our side. He was always a problem, even as a baby. I knew he'd get me into trouble one day!'

CHAPTER... ...SEVEN

It took the clean-up crew more than four hours to deactivate the SAG-11s and remove the gunk from the walls of the training zone.

Zac had waited impatiently the whole time, pacing up and down the corridor. Leon sat on the floor with his tool kit, fiddling with the FF-Matrix.

Finally, the head of the clean-up crew emerged from the training zone, holding Zac's slightly sticky ID card.

Zac took it gratefully. 'Thanks,' he said. 'Leon, we need to get going. I still have to track down Agent Test Tube, and I'm running out of time!'

Leon and Zac took the lift back up to the Advanced Research Lab on Level 27.

When the lift doors opened, Zac and Leon pulled out their ID cards and prepared to have their faces scanned again.

Once they got past security, Zac and Leon ducked around a corner.

Leon carefully fixed the FF-Matrix onto Zac's back, and then checked to see if anyone was around. 'It's clear,' he hissed.

Zac punched the FF-Matrix selections into his SpyPad.

Instantly, the holographic micro-pulses transformed him into a grey-haired man in a white lab coat.

'OK, you are Agent Screwdriver,' Leon whispered to Zac as they hurried down the corridor towards the lab. 'You're visiting from the Hollywood office. Just don't forget the geek phrases I taught you that

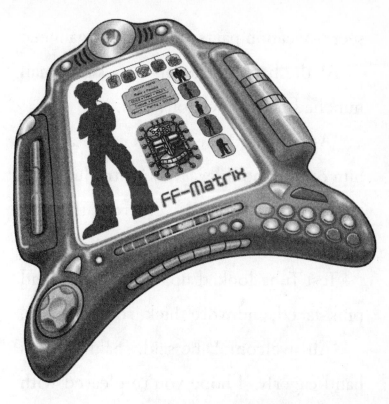

time. And remember to put on an American accent!'

Leon led Zac over to Agent Test Tube. They walked carefully through a maze of shelves filled with electronic testing gear, secret weapon parts and new spy gadgets.

At the back of the lab sat a short man hunched over a mess of wires.

'Agent Test Tube,' said Leon, tapping him on the shoulder. 'May I introduce you to, er, Agent Screwdriver, from the GIB Hollywood office?'

Test Tube looked up. He was bald and pink-faced, and wore thick, round glasses.

'Ah, welcome!' he said, shaking Zac's hand eagerly. 'I hope you're pleased with what you've seen.'

'Oh, yes,' drawled Zac in a thick American accent. 'I love your work! I read your article on Vector Bosons in the June issue of *Fundamental Particle Physics* magazine. I found it fascinating, especially the section where you argued against the old formula for calculating Photonic Spin.'

Behind Test Tube, Leon quickly gave Zac the thumbs up.

'Tremendous!' beamed Test Tube. He looked delighted that Zac had read his work. 'I'm interested to know, Agent Screwdriver, what you think about my idea that Theory of Super-Symmetry predicts the existence of particles like sleptons and neutralinos?'

Zac's mind went blank. *What the ...?*

But luckily Leon came to the rescue. He cleared his throat loudly, and said,

'Agent Test Tube, Sleptons and neutralinos aren't nearly as important as the Intelligent Jelly Corrosive Acid Bomb you've been working on! Why don't you tell Agent Screwdriver all about it?'

CHAPTER... ...EIGHT

Zac held his breath while he waited to see if Test Tube would take the bait.

But the scientist seemed happy to ramble on about his latest invention.

'Absolutely!' he squealed. 'Well, the Intelli-Jelly is based on the Portuguese Man-o-War jelly fish. I've built a robotic version from experimental high-flex plastic. And instead of poison sacs filled with venom, the Intelli-Jelly has sacs of metal-melting sulphuric acid!'

'Wow!' said Zac, forcing a smile. Inside, he was feeling nervous. *It sounds like an extremely dangerous weapon,* he thought to himself.

'I know,' said Test Tube, nodding happily. He walked over to a cabinet and gestured at two lumpy, jelly-like blobs.

'I designed it to locate enemy ships and clamp onto the hull. The Intelli-Jelly then releases its acid to burn a hole underneath and sink the target vessels! And because my invention is robotic, it can also live, move and attack out of water.'

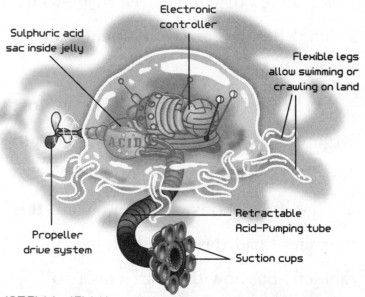

Sulphuric acid
sac inside jelly

Electronic
controller

Flexible legs
allow swimming or
crawling on land

ACID

Propeller
drive system

Retractable
Acid-Pumping tube

Suction cups

INTELLI-JELLY - (INTELLIGENT JELLY CORROSIVE ACID BOMB)

'That's amazing, Agent Test Tube!' said Zac, trying to keep his voice light. 'In fact, it sounds like something BIG would be very interested in.'

Test Tube's grin was suddenly gone. 'Screwdriver,' the scientist spluttered,

'I'm insulted that you'd even suggest such a thing! Besides, at the moment I have a small problem.'

'What's that?' asked Zac, almost forgetting his accent. He leant in close to Test Tube. 'What kind of a problem?'

Test Tube shook his head. 'Well, this morning I had three Intelli-Jellies in my cabinet…but now there are only two!'

Zac glanced at Leon, but before he could say anything, he suddenly felt a squishy lump land hard on his head.

Zac reached up and felt a cold, smooth suction pad the size of a football. Slimy tentacles reached down over his ears and wrapped around his neck.

'The missing Intelli-Jelly!' Test Tube gasped, looking at Zac's head.

It had dropped from the ceiling and clamped onto Zac's skull!

'How do I get it off?' Zac yelled, pulling desperately at the suction pads. His holographic disguise flickered, and then disappeared.

Leon shook Test Tube by the shoulders. 'In 30 seconds the Intelli-Jelly will release its acid!' Leon shouted. 'Tell us how to release the suckers – or Zac's head will dissolve!'

'I don't know!' Test Tube stammered, and then gasped. 'Oh my…where did Agent Screwdriver go?!'

Keep cool, Zac told himself, his mind racing. *Just think...*He looked around frantically, and then grabbed a large syringe with a long needle from nearby. *Perfect!*

Zac took a deep breath, and then gently poked the needle into the Intelli-Jelly. He pierced the acid sac and sucked the deadly liquid into the syringe.

'Zac, be careful!' Leon said shakily.

Zac drained the acid sac and pulled the needle out. He threw it into the chemical waste bin nearby. Then Zac grabbed a boring-looking textbook from the bench and whacked the Intelli-Jelly.

The deflated gadget fell off Zac's head and shattered on the floor of the lab.

'I'm so sorry!' whimpered Test Tube. 'I can't believe the Intelli-Jelly did that!'

Zac ran his hands through his hair, trying to fix it up. He hated it when his hair got messed up.

'I *can* believe it,' he said, feeling annoyed. 'Someone has been after me since my meeting with Agent Big Boss!'

He glared at the shattered plastic on the ground. *It must have been programmed to target me,* he realised. *It didn't go for anyone else. But who would have the security clearance to set it to attack one of GIB's own agents?*

Then suddenly, Zac had an idea. He grabbed a nearby pair of tweezers and went over to the Intelli-Jelly. He carefully dug around in the broken plastic until he found what he was looking for.

'Ah-ha!' he said, standing up and holding the brain chip carefully. 'I think I know how we can find out who programmed the Intelli-Jelly to attack me,' he said. 'Test Tube, help me upload this brain chip to your computer.'

His hands shaking, Test Tube gripped the tweezers and gently placed the brain chip in the analysis tray of his computer.

'You're right. The Intelli-Jelly records the personal identity code of the last agent to program it. It might take a while to decode it, though,' said Test Tube, tapping away at the keyboard.

'You've got to hurry,' said Zac. 'We're running out of time. The global back-up is only an hour away!'

Leon and Zac leant over Test Tube's shoulder as he scrolled through page after page of codes. The clock was ticking, but the decoding was taking ages.

'Have you found anything yet?' asked Leon anxiously.

'Almost,' said Test Tube. 'I'm just confirming the decoded identification now.'

A green box flashed up on the screen. Test Tube leant forward, a strange look on his face.

'Oh dear,' he said, shaking his head. 'The computer has made a mistake. This has never happened before, but I can't see how it could be *him*...'

Leon nudged past Test Tube and examined the screen. His jaw fell open, and he turned to stare at Zac.

'You won't believe this,' Leon gulped, 'but the personal identity code belongs to…Agent Big Boss!'

CHAPTER...
...NINE

'The perfect cover for a mole,' Zac said. 'The one person we'd never investigate!'

'What does this mean?!' whispered Agent Test Tube.

'It means that you're off my list of suspects,' said Zac, 'and that I've got to get back down to Level 62!'

Leon and Zac raced down the hallway towards the lifts. As fast as they could, they scanned their IDs and ran through the security checks.

How will I get inside the office? thought Zac quickly, as the doors closed. *I need the element of surprise!*

'Leon, do you have any friends who are security agents on Level 62?' he asked.

'Yup,' said Leon. 'Why?'

'Send them a message now,' said Zac, 'and tell them we're coming. Make sure you can trust them, though. I need to get into the office before Big Boss finds out we're onto him.'

'Got it,' said Leon with a nod.

When the lift doors opened, a huge security guard was waiting for them.

'It's OK,' the guard said in a low voice. 'Come with me.'

'This is Agent Brick Wall,' Leon whispered.

Brick Wall pushed Zac and Leon past the metal detector and security scanners.

'There's a few of us on standby,' he said quietly. 'We'll wait outside the office with Leon while you go in. Call out *mole patrol* if you need back-up.'

Zac nodded, his heart thumping wildly. *How much time do I have?* he wondered.

Only 13 minutes until the back-up begins!

Brick Wall pressed the buzzer next to the heavy steel door. After a moment, the door slid open.

'Sorry to interrupt, sir,' said Agent Brick Wall. 'Agent Rock Star is here with an urgent update.'

'Agent Rock Star, here *now*?' exclaimed Big Boss, sounding annoyed.

Zac walked into the office. He heard the distinct click of the door locking behind him. 'Hello, sir.'

'Oh, er...Rock Star,' he said awkwardly. His voice sounded weird. Was it slightly too high? 'Good to see you again. You have an urgent mole update for me, then?'

'That's right,' Zac said, glancing around the office.

It looked untidy, as though some sort of scuffle had taken place. One of the office chairs was lying on its side.

Zac's spy senses tingled. He looked up at the air-conditioning vent, and noticed that all four screws were now missing.

'While I've been hunting the mole,' Zac said to Big Boss, 'the mole's been hunting me. I dodged a sticky situation with some SAG-11s. And I almost got a new hairstyle from an acid-squirting Intelli-Jelly.'

'That's terrible!' said Big Boss, looking nervous. 'So, have you found out who the mole is?'

Zac was just about to reply when he saw something strange.

There was half a banana plugged into the computer! A glowing, plastic banana that made a strange buzzing sound...

Zac knew instantly that the banana was a camouflaged ScavMod.

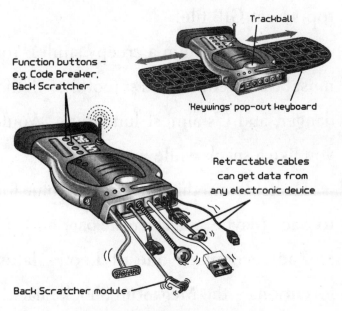

Trackball

Function buttons –
e.g. Code Breaker,
Back Scratcher

'Keywings' pop-out keyboard

Retractable cables
can get data from
any electronic device

Back Scratcher module

Scavenger Module (ScavMod)

And the other half of it is probably the stolen TeraStick!

Zac tore his eyes away from the ScavMod, but it was too late. Big Boss had seen him looking.

Zac was certain Big Boss was the mole. He was getting ready to download every top-secret GIB file!

Big Boss shot him a creepy smile. 'You must be starved,' he said smoothly. 'All that danger, and it's almost lunchtime. Would you like a snack while we chat?'

He held something wrapped in blue foil to Zac. 'Maybe … a *chocolate* bar?'

Zac recognised one of Leon's latest inventions – the MegaStun Shock Snack!

Electrodes deliver
a non-lethal
100,000 volt shock

Air-sensor
activates shock

WARNING: MAY
CONTAIN TRACES
OF STUN

MEGA
NUTS
High Energy Snack Bar

Delicious
choc-nut casing

MegaStun Shock Snack

Zac knew that if he touched the end that
Agent Big Boss was holding out to him,
he'd be zapped unconscious with 100,000
volts of electricity. Zac had to outsmart Big
Boss somehow!

In a split second, Zac bounded onto the

desk like a cat, and kicked the MegaStun bar out of the GIB head's hand. *Lucky I'm wearing rubber-soled sneakers*, he thought to himself.

'No!' Agent Big Boss cried out.

The Shock Snack landed on the office carpet, sparking dangerously.

Before Big Boss could do anything, Zac stomped one heel down on the ScavMod. Spotting the TeraStick, he crushed his other heel into it, shattering it easily. Mashed banana spurted everywhere.

'Mole patrol!' yelled Zac. And then he dived straight at Agent Big Boss!

CHAPTER... ...TEN

Zac rolled around the office floor with Big Boss in a headlock. He could hear Leon, Agent Test Tube and some security guards shouting and pounding on the locked metal door.

Then suddenly, there was a **ZAAP!** Agent Big Boss had rolled right on top of the sparking MegaStun Shock Snack!

Big Boss squealed and twitched, trying desperately to get away.

Zac looked up, breathing heavily. Then he got the shock of his life. Big Boss had turned into a *girl*!

And not just any girl, thought Zac angrily, getting to his feet. *It's Caz! She's been using a stolen FF-Matrix!*

Caz was BIG's most cunning spy, and the only enemy that Zac had never captured. She always managed to get away. But not this time!

Then Zac heard a sound coming from underneath the desk. He sprinted around the desk and looked under it.

There, gagged, handcuffed and tied up,

was the *real* Agent Big Boss!

Zac breathed a sigh of relief. The head of GIB wasn't a mole after all! He tugged the gag free.

'She…came from…nowhere,' gasped Agent Big Boss, 'and zapped me!'

Fists were still thumping on the door. Zac hit the lock control and the security guards burst into the room.

'You must have been out since late last night, sir,' said Zac, helping the head of GIB up as guards swarmed around them.

'Caz assumed your identity. She must have controlled the attacks on me from your office. But don't worry, everything is under control now. Caz is right here…'

Zac trailed off as he turned to where Caz had been lying.

But the evil agent had disappeared! Zac glanced up at the roof and saw a flash of Caz's shoe as she scrambled up the air-conditioning vent.

'She's gone up there,' he yelled at the guards.

A GIB guard sent out a message. 'Intruder alert! Secure all vents!'

The security guards bolted out of the office towards the lifts.

Agent Big Boss turned to Zac and Leon. 'Embarrassing as it is for the head of GIB to be caught off guard,' he said with a tired smile, 'I need to thank you. You managed to thwart BIG's attempt to destroy GIB.'

Big Boss poked at the mashed remains of the ScavMod and TeraStick. 'I'm going to order a full investigation into how our security was breached by BIG. I just don't know how this happened.'

A moment later, Big Boss' intercom crackled urgently. 'The BIG intruder has just escaped out of the fire door on Level 1!'

Zac's mouth dropped open, but before he could say anything, his SpyPad beeped.

You have a pool to clean!

AGENT BUM SMACK

Later that afternoon, Zac was scooping leaves out of the pool.

I hate cleaning the pool, he thought, feeling tired and bored.

One minute I'm saving GIB, the next minute I'm covered in pool slime!

Then he heard a car beeping madly. Zac turned and saw Leon zooming across the lawn in the Triox.

'Hey!' Zac said. 'Come to help me clean the pool?'

'Not quite,' Leon grinned, hopping out of the Triox. 'I do have a surprise for you, though. Meet the Aqua-Blitzer Pool Hygiene Robot, one of my latest inventions!'

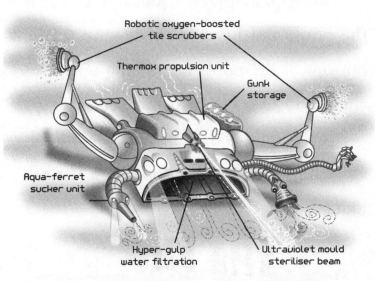

Robotic oxygen-boosted tile scrubbers

Thermox propulsion unit

Gunk storage

Aqua-ferret sucker unit

Hyper-gulp water filtration

Ultraviolet mould steriliser beam

AQUA–BLITZER Heavy Duty Pool Hygiene Robot

Leon placed a very strange-looking contraption on the ground, and it scuttled towards Zac. It was covered in brushes, scrubbers, suckers and cleaning snouts.

Zac laughed. 'Awesome!'

The Aqua-Blitzer squeaked towards the pool, and jumped in. It sank to the bottom of the pool, vacuuming up leaves and leaving a trail of gleaming tiles.

'Just don't tell mum,' Zac grinned, stretching out by the pool on a banana lounge.

...**THE END**...

Your mission: read all the books
in the Zac Power series ...

 POISON ISLAND
 DEEP WATERS
 FROZEN FEAR
 MIND GAMES

 NIGHT RAID
 TOMB OF DOOM
 LUNAR STRIKE
 SUDDEN DROP

 BLOCKBUSTER
 SHOCKWAVE
 HIGH RISK
 UNDERCOVER

END

READING
>>> ON

For freebies, downloads
and info about other
Zac Power books, go to

www.zacpower.com